MYSTERY IN THE OLD CAVE

Mystery
in the Old Cave

By HELEN FULLER ORTON

ILLUSTRATED BY ROBERT DOREMUS

J. B. Lippincott Company
PHILADELPHIA AND NEW YORK

Library of Congress catalog card number 50-14371

Contents

MYSTERY IN THE OLD CAVE

1.   The Sugarhouse

ANDY DRAPER woke up one morning in October and saw the sunshine streaming in at the window.

"Jeepers! It must be late!" he thought.

But a moment later he realized that it didn't matter, for this was Saturday. He jumped out of bed and ran to the window.

The grass and shrubs glistened with white frost— the first frost of the fall. Andy dressed quickly and ran downstairs, where his sister Joan was already eating breakfast.

"Look, Joan! There was a frost last night!" he exclaimed, as he took his place at the table. "Let's go to the woods and see if any hickory nuts have fallen off the trees."

"All right. I'd like to," said Joan. "Mother has taken the car and gone to the village to do the marketing. She didn't leave anything special for us to do, so we may as well gather nuts."

Ponto, their dog, looked up from his place on the floor. He had been waiting for Andy the last hour and now went over to the boy's chair.

"Morning, Ponto!" said Andy, scratching him behind the ears. Satisfied, Ponto went back to his place to wait.

Andy drank his orange juice and began on his oatmeal. His name was really Andrew, but everyone called him Andy for short. Joan's name couldn't be shortened, but sometimes it was lengthened to Joanie.

This was the first time the Drapers had lived up in the country in the fall. Usually they spent the summer vacation on this farm in Vermont on which Mother had once lived, and had gone back to New York when vacation was over.

This year, their father had come home one night

with news. "How would you like to stay up here on the farm this winter? I have a chance to rent our apartment to some friends from the West. They would greatly like to have it, for they can't find a vacant one."

"But you couldn't come home every night," Joan protested.

"No, but I'd come every week-end."

"I think it would be wonderful to stay here one winter," Mother had said.

"Gee! It would be grand," said Andy. "Would we have to go to school if we stay here?"

"Surely," Mother had replied. "In the school bus to that big school on the main road."

"I'd love it," Joan agreed.

"We'll stay then, since you are all in favor of it," Father had said.

And now they had been enjoying this fine old place since the Fourth of July, and the time had come for nuts to be gathered.

Breakfast over, Andy said, "Let's get going, Joan. Come on, Ponto."

The dog jumped up eagerly. He knew that on a morning when the children didn't go off on that big bus, something interesting would happen.

Wagging his tail joyously, Ponto hurried out and waited in the side yard. When Andy and Joan were ready, they left a note on the table for Mother, "We've gone to the woods for hickory nuts."

From their house, the land sloped up to a high ridge toward the West. So their whole farm was a beautiful hillside.

Andy went to the south wing of the house and came back with two small tin pails. "We need these for the nuts," he said, giving one to Joan.

They went through the garden, then through the gate in the picket fence and came to the hillside.

A beautiful sight it was, with small evergreen trees dotting the slope.

"How pretty the world is this morning, with the white frost sparkling!" exclaimed Joan, as they walked across the hillside.

They didn't hurry, but stopped once in a while to watch a bird or a squirrel or a rabbit.

Joan was nine, going on ten, as she always said when asked her age. Andrew was nearly two years older and a few inches taller.

"I'll bet this frost has made a lot of nuts fall off the trees," said Andy. "The first frost always loosens some of them."

When near the woods, he broke into a run. Several tall hickory trees stood at the edge of the woods, among the maples and beeches.

"Just see all the nuts on the ground!" he shouted.

"Hurrah for Jack Frost!" exclaimed Joan.

Ponto, who had been chasing a rabbit, came up to see what the excitement was about. He sniffed at some of the nuts, but they didn't interest him much, so he ran off after a bird.

Scattered on the ground were dozens of the small hard-shelled nuts, their outer shucks still on. Andy looked up. "Just see how many are still on the trees," he said.

"What shall we do with these on the ground?" Joan asked.

"We'd better put some boards down and lay the nuts on them to dry. Some day we'll shuck them and take them to the house for winter."

They found some old boards near by and laid them on the ground side by side. Then they picked up the nuts and put them on the boards in neat rows.

Joan said, "I wish the hickory trees weren't so tall, then you could climb them and shake the limbs. The nuts would fall off and we could gather them all right away."

"We'll have to wait," said Andy. "I never could climb those trees. They go straight up about thirty feet before there is a single limb. Let's go up to the old sugarhouse."

It was an old gray building that stood at the edge of the woods some distance beyond the hickory trees. In times past it had been used when folks were making maple sugar.

They had not gone far when they heard a chattering behind them. They turned around and saw a squirrel running toward the boards where they had placed the nuts. They watched him take up one in his paws, chuck it between his teeth and start off toward a big tree.

"Oh, dear! Are those squirrels going to take the nuts we gathered?" Joan exclaimed.

Ponto gave chase; and the squirrel had to drop that nut and scurry up a tree without it.

"Well done, Ponto!" said Andy. "Well done!"

"But as soon as we are gone that squirrel will go back there," sighed Joan.

"Maybe we'll have to think of some good place to take them," said Andy.

They went on toward the sugarhouse. It was an empty building now, but had been the scene of much activity and fun in former times, when the maple trees had been tapped in the spring and sugaring-off time came.

Andy pushed the bolt, opened the door, and they entered. The building had only one large room. There was a huge fireplace at one end. At the other end was a wide scaffold or platform across the entire end of the room, about ten feet from the floor. It was called the hayloft; and the floor of it was covered with hay. A ladder stood against it, so people could climb up there.

Men had sometimes slept there when, in harvest time, there were extra helpers to do the work on the farm.

Joan went straight to the cupboard built against the front wall beside the door. She reached for the cooky jar in which they kept cookies or doughnuts on hand for snacks.

"Have one?" she asked, holding out the cooky jar.

"I'll have two," said Andy.

Joan took two herself. She had brought them up the week before. Andy went to the window in the back wall of the building and tried to pull it open. It was a window that swung in on hinges instead of sliding up and down.

Tug with all his might, he couldn't move it even a little. Joan came back there. "Why fuss with it?" she asked. "No one will ever want to open that window."

"Someone might. If there was ever a fire, someone

might want to get out quick. Or there might be some other reason for wanting to get out the window instead of the door."

The truth was that Andy never liked to give up. If he started a thing, he liked to finish it. He found in a corner a strong iron chisel with a sharp end. With that he was able to start the window, then he gave a big pull and swung it in.

"There! I knew I could do it," he declared.

The window was wider than it was high. One could easily crawl through it when it was open.

Back of the building and reaching up to the high cliff at the top of the hill, there were many evergreens and some other trees, making thick woods.

Andy pulled himself up on the window sill, then dropped down to the ground. He knew that by walking up through those woods one would come to the foot of the cliff, but it was a wild rocky place and he had never done it.

Joan stood looking out. "It's a scary place," she said. "Let's go back."

Andy took his time about it, for he didn't like Joan to think she could boss him; but before long he clambered back, closed the window and fastened it tight with the wooden catch that held it shut.

They soon started back to the house, after he had fastened the door at the front of the building.

"Where's Ponto?" Joan asked, when they had gone part way across the hillside.

Andy whistled for the dog, but no dog came running, as he usually did at that call.

"Where can he be?" asked Joan, distress in her voice. "Could he have gone home ahead of us?"

Andy whistled again. They heard Ponto barking somewhere up in the woods beyond the sugarhouse.

Soon the barks changed to yelps of pain.

"Oh, dear!" cried Joan. "Is someone hurting Ponto?"

Andy started to go back, but just then Ponto came in sight around the corner of the sugarhouse, whimpering and limping.

"Some stranger must be up there. Ponto never barks at someone he knows," Andy declared.

"Poor Ponto," said Joan, bending over him and stroking him. "Did someone kick you?"

"I'm going back there and see if I can find who did it," said Andy. And he was off on the run.

Joan waited there with Ponto. She could see that the leg wasn't broken, but it evidently pained the dog badly.

When Andy came back, he told her, "That window was open. Someone must have been up on the loft when we were in the sugarhouse; and he must have gone out by the window as soon as we came away."

"Who could it have been?" asked Joan. "Anyhow, he must have been a mean man if he kicked Ponto."

2.   The Stranger

WHILE ANDY and Joan were having a fine time gathering nuts and going to the old sugarhouse that Saturday, down in the village a half-mile away another boy, Philip Ramsay, was busy at something quite different.

Phil was living with his mother's cousin, a man named John Davison. Before she died that summer, his mother had said to him, "Cousin John has promised to give you a home till you are through school. I hope you'll try to please him."

"I'll do my best," Phil had promised.

"I've left some money to Cousin John to cover the expense you will be to him for food and clothes," she had said.

Phil had tried hard to please Cousin John ever since he had come there from the town where he lived, fifty miles away. But no matter how hard he tried, he was always being scolded.

The two of them lived in a fine old mansion, one that had once been a beautiful place, but was now shabby and unpainted. Phil liked the place, even though he was put in the smallest bedroom of all. His tiny room was at the back of the house, while large rooms at the front were left vacant.

They had just finished their breakfast of cold oatmeal and dry bread that Saturday when Phil ventured to ask, "Uncle John, may I go to the woods and gather hickory nuts today? There will be some on the ground, for there was a frost last night."

It had been agreed that he would call the cousin Uncle John. It seemed to Phil more natural because his mother's cousin was a man of sixty.

Uncle John looked across the table at the twelve-year-old lad and shook his head.

"No," he said. "There's something more import·
ant to be done today. The yard has to be cleaned."

Ever since Phil had come there to live, Uncle John
had managed to find something to do about the place
every Saturday.

Phil didn't mind doing some work, but he was
thinking, as he finished his breakfast, "I wish I could
sometimes have a little fun on Saturday, as the other
boys do."

The oatmeal was cold every morning because the
housekeeper, Mrs. Yarby, who came a few hours each
day, always cooked it the day before. Uncle John
said there was no sense in warming it.

After breakfast, Phil went to work in the big yard,
carrying rubbish to the back of the lot and raking
leaves. He worked till his back ached and on till the
sun went down. In the evening, he did homework.

As Andy and Joan were getting off the school bus
at their house the following Monday afternoon, Andy
said, "Come in a while and play ping-pong in our
playroom, Phil."

Phil's face lighted up. "Thanks. I'd like to. Some
other day, maybe." He knew that he had to work at
cleaning the yard after school that day.

Joan sang out to her special friend Rosalind,

"Good-bye! See you in the morning!"

Andy waved his hand to the crowd and shouted, "Good-bye till tomorrow!"

The bus started on toward the village a half-mile south, where the rest of the boys and girls would get off.

Andy gave a loud whoop as he hurried up the walk, ran into the old wing of the house and threw his books down on the table.

Mother came to the door from the living-room. "Do I hear a wild Indian?" she asked.

Andy laughed. "Sorry, Mom. But it seemed good to be able to shout as loud as I wanted to, after sitting in school all day. Oh, boy! Am I hungry!"

Joan came in, having walked a bit slower. "Just think, Mother! I'm to be monitor tomorrow!"

"That's good," said Mrs. Draper with a smile. "I'm glad the teacher thinks you can be trusted with such a responsible job."

"I'm hungry too," said Joan.

"There's plenty of bread in the pantry. And there's milk and butter in the icebox. Help yourselves."

They needed no second invitation. Andy spread his bread thick with peanut butter. Joan spread hers with jam. Having finished their snack, Andy said,

"Let's go up to the woods, Sis, and gather more hickory nuts."

"May we, Mother?" asked Joan, who knew she might be told to practice her music first.

"Well, these lovely autumn days won't last forever," Mother replied. "Yes, I think it would be a good idea for you to go out in the open air."

With a whoop and a leap Andy was off the side porch bareheaded. Joan called to him, "Wait a minute till I'm ready."

And it wasn't much more than a minute before she appeared at the door in her playsuit, for Joan was quick at doing things.

The woods were a glory of color—red of maple, yellow of beech and hickory, crimson of oak. And among them all and setting them off, the green of pines and firs.

They raced over the grass, turning out when they came to one of the little fir trees that dotted the hillside. Joan could run almost as fast as Andy.

"Come, Ponto. Let's race to the woods," said Andy. Ponto seemed to understand. Though he still limped a little, he bounded ahead, glad to have some fun, after lying around the house all day.

Joan, coming along a moment later, heard Andy

shout, "Jeepers! Look what's happened!"

She hurried on. The hickory nuts they had so carefully placed on the boards were more than half gone.

"Oh-h! Those pesky squirrels!" she exclaimed.

"We might have known it," said Andy.

"Could such little animals have taken so many?" Joan asked ruefully.

"I s'pose they might if there were enough of the little rascals. They had two whole days for doing it."

Joan began to move the remaining nuts over to one side of the boards. "We'll just have to pick up more," she said. "There are lots on the ground. Why didn't they take those nuts instead of stealing the ones we worked so hard for?"

"If we leave them here, the squirrels may carry off all these," said Andy.

At that moment, they heard a chattering off through the woods. "Look!" said Joan. "Those two squirrels are telling us to go away, so they can come and get some more."

It did sound as if they were scolding. They chattered and scolded till Andy and Joan laughed heartily.

Andy threw a hickory nut over that way. One squirrel picked up the nut and started off with it toward a maple tree. Ponto gave chase, but the squirrel

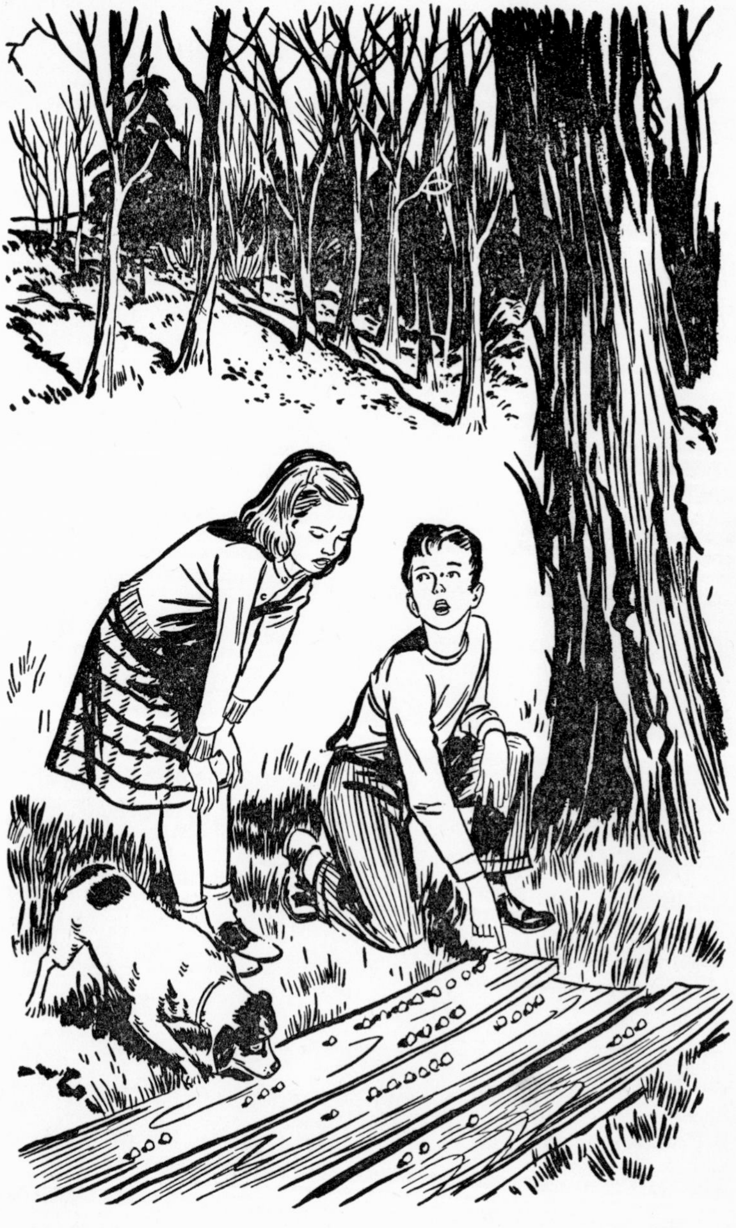

was too quick for him and got the nut safely up to a hole in a big limb, where he ducked in.

"Clever little creatures, aren't they?" said Joan.

"We'd better think of some good place to put the rest of the nuts where they are safe," said Andy.

"I have a thought," said Joan. "Couldn't we put them in the sugarhouse?"

"That's a good idea. We'll shut the door tight and fill up all the cracks, so no little thief can get in."

Andy ran home for the two little pails. "We want them for carrying nuts to the sugarhouse," he told Mother.

"Why take them to the sugarhouse? Won't nuts dry better out in the sunshine?"

"Yes, but the squirrels may carry them all off if we leave them there."

When he came back, Joan was standing very still, watching something. "Sh! Be quiet!" she said in a low tone.

They stood as still as statues while the squirrel took a nut and carried it off. He evidently told others, for three more came running to the boards.

"Jeepers! That's enough!" Andy declared. "Let's hurry and carry the rest of the nuts away."

They filled the pails and started off toward the

sugarhouse. Andy went ahead and unbolted the door. He stepped inside.

Joan was always haunted by the idea that some wild animal might choose the old building for a den. She had heard tales of how bears lived in old trappers' huts in old times. "Is there anything in there?" she asked.

"How could there be, with the door locked?"

They decided that a good place for the nuts would be in front of the old fireplace. The smooth old hearthstone was still there.

As Joan bent over to place the nuts on it, there was a rustling sound in the hay on the loft. She jumped. "Who's that?" she asked in a scared voice.

Andy went over and climbed the ladder. Two bright eyes peeked at him from a corner of the loft.

"It's only a squirrel," he said. "We must fill up all the cracks so they can't get in any more."

"Gray squirrels are awful pretty, but what pests they are!" said Joan.

They emptied the pails, then went back and forth several times for more nuts. By the time they had placed them all on the hearthstone, it was getting dark in the corners of the old building.

"We'd better go home," said Joan.

Andy looked again at the window to see that it was fastened tightly. "There's surely no one in the sugarhouse this time," he said, as he fastened the door and they walked away.

They were just coming to the hickory trees when there came a queer call from the woods back of them. "Too-whoo! Hey there!"

They could see a man coming toward them from the direction of the sugarhouse. Andy said to Joan, "You wait here. I'll go back to see what he wants."

He was a man of middle age, standing near the sugarhouse. Andy could see that he was a stranger and was shabbily dressed.

"Hey, kid! I s'pose you live around here?" asked the stranger.

"Yes, part of the time. We really live in New York."

"Oh—h!" said the man in a disappointed tone.

"Most years we're up here just in summer," Andy told him.

"I want to ask you a question," said the man, coming closer and speaking softly, as if afraid someone would hear. "You mustn't tell anyone else. Just tell me what you know about this and keep still."

Andy kept wondering what the question would be.

"Now, Sonny, do you know where there's a cave up there in the cliff?" He pointed to the cliff that rose about forty feet high a few rods back of the sugar-house.

"A cave?" said Andy, all excited. "I'd sure like to see one, but I don't know of any around here."

"Well, I've heard that there is one. I met a feller not long ago who told me all about it—a cave in the cliff, not far from the old sugarhouse," he said.

"Do you think it's still here?" asked Andy.

"That's what I want to know."

"I never saw it, Mister."

"Something must have happened to it," said the stranger. "Maybe in a big storm earth and rocks fell over the cliff and closed it up."

"Maybe that was it," said Andy. "Well, I'd better go home now."

He didn't quite like the looks of the man and wanted to get away.

As Andy hurried back toward Joan, he thought, "I'll bet he was the man who kicked Ponto the other day. I wonder why he wants to find an old cave."

"What did he want?" Joan asked.

"He's just hunting for something, but I couldn't help him any, for I don't know a thing about it."

3.   The Torn Sweater

A WEEK LATER, when Andy got off the school bus, he said, "Come on in, Phil, and have some fun in our playroom."

Phil had made up his mind that if an invitation came again, he would accept and take a chance that Uncle John wouldn't scold too much.

"Thanks, I'll come for half an hour."

Mrs. Draper sat reading a book in the living-room when the boys came in. "Mother, this is my friend, Phil Ramsay, a boy who rides to school with us," said Andy.

"I'm very glad to see you," said Mrs. Draper. "I'm always glad to meet Andy's friends."

After listening to the report of things that had happened in school, she went to the kitchen and put some sandwiches and a pitcher of milk on the dinette table.

"You must have a snack with Andy and Joan," she said to Phil, as both boys followed her.

Joan appeared in a moment and they all enjoyed the delicious sandwiches and two glasses of milk apiece.

"Thank you very much, Mrs. Draper," Phil said politely, when they had finished. "Those were dandy sandwiches."

"Come in often," she said, for she could see that he was the sort of lad she would like to have there. "Andy will show you the south wing."

Andy led the way to the large room in the old part of the house. Sunshine was streaming in at the west windows. The room contained all sorts of things for good times—a table for games, another for doing homework, bats and balls and mitts in one corner, books and magazines.

"Gee! What a pleasant room!" Phil exclaimed.

"Joan and I like it. We have lots of fun here," Andy agreed.

The two boys played ping-pong. Joan sat at the table and drew a map. The sound of the little white balls being struck back and forth was exciting and pleasant for the next half-hour. Andy won, for he had had much practice.

"You did fine, seeing it was your first time," he said to Phil. "Come often and get a lot of practice."

Suddenly Phil glanced at the clock. "Jeepers! I must be going," he said.

Joan had been drawing the map, but one ear had been on the game. When Andy came back after walking down to the road with his visitor, she said, "Phil learns quickly. He'll soon beat you if you don't watch out."

Phil ran the last part of the way to the village and arrived breathless at the side door of Uncle John's house, meaning to say he was sorry for being late.

Uncle John was waiting for him. "Where have you been all this time?" he demanded. "The bus came through an hour ago."

"I—one of the boys asked me to go home with him for a little while. I didn't think about its being so long."

"Didn't think! Didn't think!" And he gave Phil a cuff on one cheek. "Maybe you'll think another time."

Phil reeled away from the blow. "I—I'm sorry, sir. We were having such a good time playing ping-pong that the time went fast."

"Playing ping-pong, eh? What right have you to stop after school and play anything when there is work to be done? For that you shall start cleaning the cellar this very day and keep at it every day after school. And when that is done, you'll whitewash it."

"Yes, sir."

"And remember, you'll not waste your time playing after school. Do you hear?"

"Yes, Uncle John."

Phil recalled what his mother had told him: "I haven't seen Cousin John for several years. He used to be a bit severe with his own son, who ran away. I hope he'll be kinder to another lad. Anyway, he is the only relative I can think of for you to live with till you finish school."

Phil often thought of those words and the ones that followed, "So, both for your own sake and to please me, try to get along with Cousin John, even if you sometimes think he is severe."

A few minutes later, Phil was in the big cellar

looking around and trying to decide what to tackle first, of all the piles of junk he saw in that huge place.

Having decided to take out some trash from one of the dark corners, he hung a lantern on a nail, peeled off his jacket and went to work.

His mother had always said that boys should have plenty of time for play and sport, but should also learn to be useful. So Phil had never thought of protesting against doing his share to keep the place clean and neat, but he did feel that it wasn't fair never to be allowed to play as the other boys did.

The corner was full of old tin pails and pans and basins, old rakes and hoes and kettles. "These things must have been here for years," thought Phil, as he handled the old rusty things. "Why didn't Uncle John throw them away instead of cluttering up the cellar with them?"

He kept pulling things out of the pile and putting the worst ones in one place and the better ones in another.

He had almost finished that corner and was about to go upstairs when he felt something pull and heard a ripping sound.

"Jeepers! I hope my sweater isn't torn," he said.

Trying to find out what had happened, he found that a broken wire had caught in his sweater and made a long tear in the arm of it.

"Oh! I'll have to have a new sweater," he thought, as he tried to pull out the rough end of the wire.

Finally he got it out and discovered a long jagged tear.

He picked up the lantern and went slowly upstairs. He meant to speak of the tear at once and say, "I'm sorry, Uncle John."

Before he could say the first word, the man's eyes fell on the ugly tear. And there began a flood of words that made Phil fairly tremble.

"Why should you tear your sweater?" he demanded. "Careless! How did you do that?"

"It caught on a wire while I was picking up some trash. I'm sorry, Uncle John."

"Sorry! As if that would mend a tear like this. Careless! For that you shall go to bed with nothing but bread and water for supper."

"All right. But may I have a new sweater? I'll still wear this when doing dirty work, but I'd like a good one for school."

"You'll still wear it to school. Of course you'll not have a new one. It can be mended so it will do."

They ate supper in silence. Uncle John had a good meal of chops and baked potatoes which the house-keeper had prepared before she left. Phil had a glass of water and two slices of bread without any butter.

After supper Uncle John said, "Let me have the sweater. I've mended my own clothes many times. I guess I can mend that one."

Reluctantly Phil took the sweater off and handed it to Uncle John. Then he went to his room and finished his homework.

"I'll not wear that sweater to school," he kept thinking.

But he did. To be sure, the edges of the tear were drawn together, but it was roughly mended and the unsightly spot showed almost as far as the sweater could be seen.

On the bus, going to school the next morning, he had his jacket over it. And when in school the other boys took off their jackets, he kept his on, though he was too warm.

The teacher said to him, "Take off your jacket, Philip. It is hot in the room this morning."

Reluctantly he took it off; but he couldn't get his thoughts off the ugly tear.

"Not one of the other boys is wearing a mended sweater," was his bitter thought. "Why should I have to endure such a thing?"

Then he turned in his seat, so as to keep that sleeve out of sight.

4. The Red Pencil

AFTER SCHOOL every day that week, Andy and Joan ran across the hillside to the hickory trees.

They gathered the nuts that had fallen to the ground, carried them to the sugarhouse and laid them on the boards to dry.

It was an Indian summer day. Sunshine lay softly over hillside and woodland. The trees were gay with autumn leaves. They filled their pails with nuts and carried them to the sugarhouse. When they had put them all on the floor with the others, Joan opened a bag of cookies she had brought along.

"Have some," she said, holding out the bag.

They each ate one. Then she put the dozen that were left, in the cooky jar in the cupboard beside the door.

"They'll come in handy sometime, when we're hungry," she said.

Twice that week Andy asked Phil to stop at their place after school, but each time Phil said, "Thank you. I'd like to, but I can't today."

He didn't explain that every night that week he would be kept busy cleaning the cellar and there wasn't much chance that he would ever be allowed to go to anyone's home.

When the bus stopped for Andy and Joan to get off, Phil looked longingly at the old wing and thought of its cheery playroom.

The day Andy and Joan went to gather the last of the hickory nuts, there were still some on the trees, but Joan suggested, "Let's leave them for the squirrels and chipmunks."

"Sure," Andy agreed.

They filled their pails with the nuts on the ground

and started off toward the sugarhouse, glad that their task was so nearly done.

Andy pulled the door open and went in first. "Everything's all right. Come in," he said.

Joan stepped quickly over the threshold and walked over to the hearthstone, where they had spread the nuts. She looked down ruefully, then exclaimed, "Oh, Andy! The nuts are half gone."

Andy hurried over there. "Gee whillikens!" he exclaimed.

"After all our hard work!" Joan said. "Could squirrels carry off so many?"

"Jeepers!" he exclaimed. "I stuffed up all the cracks, so none could get in."

Joan went to the cupboard and took down the cooky jar. She held it out, saying, "Have one, Andy."

"I surely will. It's hard work gathering nuts. Makes one hungry."

He put his hand in the jar. "Where have they all gone?" he asked. "There aren't any left!"

"Why, Andy! I put a dozen there."

"I know you did, but they're gone now."

Joan began to put the nuts they had brought on the floor where the others had been.

Andy said, "Joan, squirrels never took all those nuts. Someone has been here and stolen them."

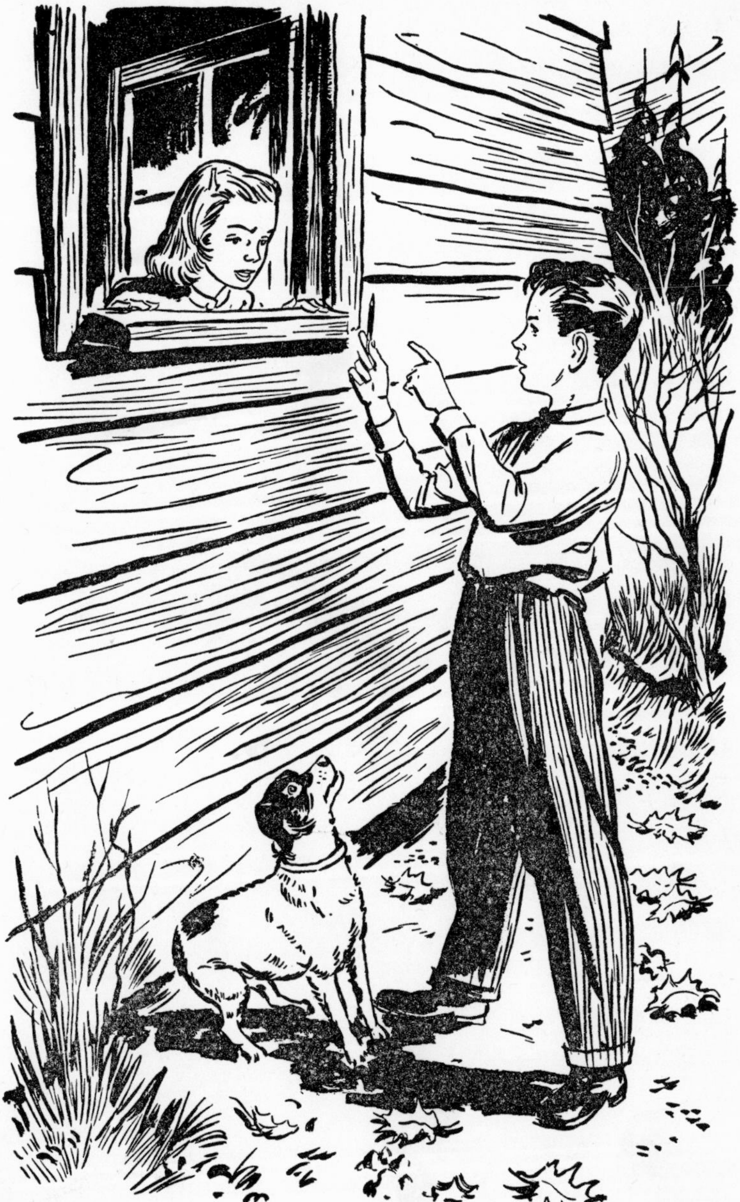

"Why, the very idea! Do you think anyone would? Folks around here don't steal."

He went on, "The same person took the cookies."

While they were busy with the nuts, Joan thought she heard footsteps crunching on the pebbles.

"Who can that be, Andy?"

"Where?"

"At the back of the sugarhouse."

Andy hurried on tiptoe to the window; but by the time he had turned the catch and pulled the window open, there was no one in sight.

"I guess you just imagined you heard footsteps," he said. "Your ears are too good, Joan."

"I did truly hear something," she said.

Andy went back to close the window, but first he leaned out and looked on the ground.

"Jeepers!" he exclaimed. "Someone has been here."

"How large are the footprints?" Joan asked. "Was it a boy or a man?"

"I don't see any footprints. The ground is so dry there wouldn't be any. But the person dropped something out here."

Before Joan could reach the window, Andy had climbed out and was picking up something. He didn't come back at once, but stood peering off through the woods.

"Do you see anyone?" she asked.

"No, but I think this was dropped here not long ago."

He held up a lead pencil, one about half used. "That isn't one of ours," he said.

"Of course not," Joan agreed. "That is red. Ours are yellow. That is round. We get six-sided ones."

Andy climbed back through the window and fastened it tight. Then he said, "Someone is coming to this sugarhouse. That is as plain as the nose on your face."

"And that person has carried most of our hickory nuts away," said Joan.

"Tell you what—we'd better take them down to the house," said Andy. "With the squirrels and chipmunks taking those we put under the trees and someone—probably a grown man—stealing those we leave here, we won't have any nuts left to eat this winter."

Joan looked worried for a moment. "After all our hard work," she said.

"There's no other way," Andy assured her. "Let's get busy."

They filled the pails with nuts and carried them back across the hillside, down to the house.

"Why are you bringing the hickory nuts down

before the shucks are off?" asked Mother, when they came up on the back porch.

"If we leave them on the ground the squirrels and chipmunks carry them off; and someone has taken most of those we put in the sugarhouse. Can't we put them somewhere in the house?"

"You might put them in the south wing. Lay newspapers down on the floor."

He and Joan put them on the floor of the main room, off in one corner, then went back for more. And they kept at it till the sun set and shadows began to fall in the woods. Even then there were some left that couldn't be put into the last pails.

"Let's leave them," said Joan. "We can eat them when we come up here sometime in the winter."

Andy fastened the front door and they hurried home. When they had put the last nuts down on the floor and had turned on the lights, Joan looked around the room with a satisfied feeling.

There were the things they liked to play with, games, skates, Andy's baseball kit and bookshelves with their books. And there was a big table for doing their homework.

"I like this room," Joan said.

"Of course," Andy agreed. "It's a jolly place. I

don't know what we'd do without this old wing."

Father had come home early that day. He was sitting under one of the lights in the living-room, reading his paper.

Mother asked Andy to go to the store on an errand —to get some orange juice and cornflakes for breakfast.

While waiting for his change, he noticed something that made him excited. The storekeeper was using a red pencil, just like the one he had found back of the sugarhouse.

"Do you always use that kind of pencil?" Andy asked.

"Yes; I don't have these for sale. Other people seem to like other kinds better, but I'm fond of this kind, so I always keep them on hand."

Andy started to ask: "Have you been up to the old sugarhouse today?" but he knew perfectly well that the storekeeper hadn't, for he was always in the store all day.

"Someone stole one of his pencils and went up to the sugarhouse and dropped it," Andy decided.

5.   Phil's New Job

THE LAST WEEK of October came. The leaves had fallen from the trees. The nuts had all been gathered. Hallowe'en was just around the corner.

When Joan got off the school bus on Monday, she said to her chum, Rosalind, "Come home with me and we'll do our homework together."

"I'd love to," said Rosalind, and she followed Joan off the bus.

Andy ran up the walk, after saying good-bye to the bunch as usual.

After a snack of sandwiches and milk, the girls went into the south wing. While doing their homework at the big table, Joan said, "Let's design a new dress for my doll the Princess. I know you'll have some good ideas."

With drawing pencils they set to work, then went to the box where Joan kept bits of silk and velvet of pretty colors, to select the materials.

Meanwhile, when Andy had finished his lunch, Mother asked, "How did things go at school today?"

"Grand," he replied. "It's a fine school. I like it."

"That's good," said Mother. "How would you like to go to the village and get some groceries? The car is being repaired, so I haven't been able to go down there today."

"I'd like it swell. With Joan and Rosalind playing with dolls, I'd a heap rather go to the store than stay around here."

Mother gave him the list. With a market bag hanging on his arm he went down the road whistling a merry tune.

The village had one long main street, with houses at the north end, then a few blocks of stores, then houses again. There was a row of elm trees on each side of the street and their branches met overhead. Andy always liked this street.

To his surprise, when part way to the store, he met Phil coming along with a basket of groceries. "Where can he be taking those things," Andy wondered. "It can't be to his uncle's house, for he has already passed that."

"Hello, Phil! What's the grand idea?" he asked.

"I have a job after school—helping Mr. Lane in the store."

"But I thought your uncle wouldn't let you go anywhere after school."

"He won't let me go to play, but he let me take this job when Mr. Lane offered it."

"That's just fine—only I wish you could sometimes come to our house. We'd have good times together."

"So do I, but this is much more interesting than staying at home. And it isn't hard work."

"But there can't be many folks that have their groceries delivered. Most everyone has a car. The folks drive to the store for their own things."

"Yes, most everyone. But these are going to Mrs. Woodman, who lives in that big house at the next corner. She doesn't drive a car, so she telephones her orders."

"Oh, I see."

"There are a few others that do the same. But I must get going."

"I'll wait for you. I'm going to the store."

In five minutes Phil was back, having taken the groceries to the back door of the large house. He had a happy look on his face. That was nothing strange, for Phil usually looked pleasant, but what he said surprised Andy.

"That lady gave me a dime. See!" he held it up. "I didn't expect anything, but she seemed to want me to have it, so I took it."

"She's always doing nice things for folks."

They walked to the general store, on the main street, not far from the center of the village.

"Anything more for me to do, Mr. Lane?" Phil asked.

"No, not now. If you can stay a while after closing time, you can help me put some new stock in place. The Hallowe'en things came this afternoon."

"Yes, I'll be glad to stay, if Andy will stop on his way home and tell my uncle why I'm late."

"Of course," Andy declared. "But now let's have some ice cream."

Phil's happy look changed to one of embarrassment. Andy guessed the reason.

"I have money enough for both of us," he said.

The storekeeper spoke up. "I'll treat you both," he said. "Nothing I like better than to treat boys to ice cream once in a while."

This was a general store, that kept all sorts of things. There were groceries in one part, dishes and kitchen utensils in another part, toys and games and even books in another part, shoes and sweaters and playsuits in another.

The storekeeper was a jolly man. He came over to wait on them after they had taken their places on the stools.

He always reminded Joan of Santa Claus, for he was pleasant and jolly. And he did look a bit like Santa Claus, for he was short and plump, with kindly blue eyes.

"What flavor?" he asked.

"Fudge sundae for me, thank you," said Phil.

"Chocolate and vanilla for me," said Andy.

Mr. Lane had soon placed the delicious treats before the boys. Then, as there were no customers in the store, he stayed to talk with them.

"How's school?" he asked.

"Just grand," they said together.

"Like it, eh?"

"Sure," said Phil.

"So you folks are staying up here all winter this year," he said to Andy.

"Yes."

"You can have a lot of fun on that hillside when snow comes. I remember when I was a boy, how we used to go there and have great fun."

"Did you live here then?" Phil asked.

"Yes, lived here all my life. Nicest place in the world to live. Why, I wouldn't trade this little village for your whole city of New York, with Boston and Chicago thrown in."

Andy looked in wonder at the man. "Wouldn't you really?"

"Nope. Your big cities are all right, but there are lots of things you can never have there. Take maple sugar makin' for one thing. What sport we used to have at the sugarin'-off times in that old sugarhouse!"

"So you've seen maple sugar being made!" said Phil.

"Many a time. Every spring, when the sap rose in the maple trees, the men on that farm tapped the trees and hung buckets on 'em to catch the sap."

"Oh, is that the way we get maple syrup?" asked Andy.

"Sure—sap from live maple trees. When the sunshine warms up the trees after the cold winter, the sap

begins to run up through the trunk of the tree. Your
grandpa and his helpers, Andy, would collect the sap
in barrels and take it up to the sugarhouse."

He stopped a few moments to answer the telephone.
When he came back, Phil asked, "Then what?"

"They would hang a big kettle on a pole over a
fire outside the sugarhouse, put the sap in and boil it
down till it was thick enough for maple syrup. Some
of it they would boil some more to make maple sugar."

"It must have been fun," said Phil.

"A pretty sight it was, with the people from the
village standing around and the fire lighting up their
faces."

"I'd like to have been there," said Andy.

"And a fine smell it was too," Mr. Lane went on.
"We boys could hardly wait till the boiling sap was
thick enough to be dipped out and given to us in tin
cups."

"You must have had a jolly time," said Phil.

"Indeed we did. The whole village came, boys and
girls, grown folks, even babies in their mothers' arms.
Friends and neighbors together, we did enjoy that
sugar makin'."

He was silent a moment and seemed to be thinking
of something far away and long ago.

"One time even some thieves joined us. We didn't

know they were thieves. They just seemed to be strangers who happened along and joined in the frolicking. There were two of them. One sang a song and we clapped our hands for more."

"How did you find out they were thieves?" Andy asked.

"That same week there were some robberies in the village. The men of the village traced the thieves to their hideout—a cave up in the cliff."

Andy stared, remembering the stranger asking him about a cave.

"A cave, did you say? Is there a cave around here?" asked Phil, his eyes aglow.

"Oh, yes. They recovered some of the stolen goods there, but the thieves had gone. They were caught later, I believe."

"Jeepers! I'd like to see a cave," said Phil, all excited. "Where is it?"

"I can't tell exactly. When I was your age, I used to go there often. We boys played there."

"Gee! I'd like to see it," said Andy. "Can't you tell us where we could find it?"

"The fact is, that a few years ago I tried to find it and couldn't. The entrance must have got covered up with vines and bushes. Or, maybe earth and stones have fallen down and covered up the mouth of it. I do remember that it is not so very far from your sugarhouse."

"Gee! I'm going to try to find it sometime," said Andy.

"I'll go with you," said Phil. "Why not go today?"

"Could you?" asked Andy.

"How about it, Mr. Lane?" Phil asked. "Is there anything for me to do now?"

"Nothing special. I can spare you."

"Tell us where to look for it," said Andy.

"You'd better start at your sugarhouse and walk up to the foot of the cliff, then turn south. It's rough walking there, for there are rocks and bushes and trees."

"We won't mind that," said Phil.

"You'd better take along a flashlight. If you should find the cave, you couldn't see a thing in there without a light."

"There's a flashlight in the sugarhouse," said Andy. "We'll take that. Come on, Phil."

School had closed an hour early that day, so the sun was still high.

6.   The Cave

EAGER TO BE off, the boys rushed out the door and ran up a short street toward the hillside. They walked up the hill and through the woods to the sugarhouse.

Andy took the flashlight from the cupboard and was ready to go.

"We'd better take things to dig with," said Phil. "If the mouth of the cave has been closed up we can't dig it out with our hands."

Andy went to a corner where a number of tools were stored. "Here's a pick-ax," he said. "You can take that and I'll take a spade."

They hurried up toward the cliff, going around big rocks and clumps of evergreens. The cliff looked like a wall of rock that rose forty or fifty feet high, a few rods beyond the sugarhouse.

A rabbit hopped out of the way. A squirrel crossed their path and ran up a tree, but the boys didn't stop to look at anything.

When they came to the cliff, they turned south, as the storekeeper had suggested. The rocks in the side of the cliff were of lovely colors, some light gray, some dark gray, some red, in irregular layers.

"Pretty," said Phil.

Here and there vines or bushes grew in the crevices of the rocks.

"What did Mr. Lane say the entrance of the cave was like?" Phil asked.

"He said it used to be a little jagged archway, near the bottom of the cliff, not a real arch, but something like one."

Every little while Phil would strike the side of the cliff with his pick-ax, when he came to a place where earth and stones were piled up against it.

"If rain washed dirt and stones down from above,

they might make a pile up against the cliff," he said.

"And grass might have grown over it," said Andy.

They had gone along many rods and had found no sign of an opening into the rocky side of the cliff. They were about to give up when Phil struck the pick-ax deep into a tangle of vines and bushes near a pile of rocks.

Earth and little stones rolled down. Andy moved them away with the spade. Something told the boys that this might be the place, for the sound of the pick was different. They worked like beavers.

Suddenly Phil shouted, "Here's a little hole through the rock. I'll bet this is the mouth of the cave."

They forgot that they were tired, so excited they were.

"Look, Andy! This sure is something!" Phil called out, after working a few minutes more.

Now they could both see it plainly—an opening a little like a doorway. By stooping a little they could go through it before long, when they had cleared away more dirt.

Although the sun was setting by this time, Phil said, "Let's go in and see what it's like. All my life I've wanted to see a cave."

With Phil going ahead and carrying the flashlight,

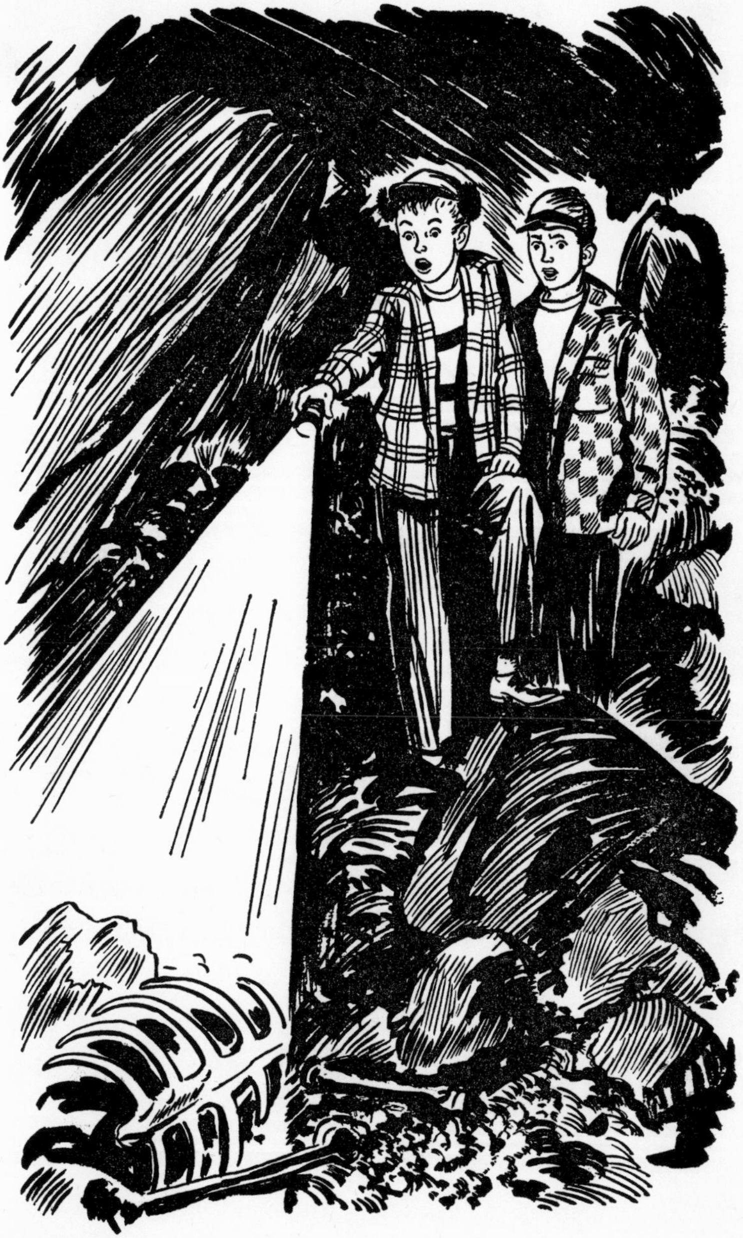

they carefully and cautiously stepped through the opening and down a little incline.

"Jeepers! Twice jeepers!" cried Phil. "Look at what we've found!"

The dim light from the opening and the flashlight showed that it was a large room underground, larger than any of the rooms at home, higher too. The walls were all of rock. The floor was solid rock.

"Gee! This is a marvel!" Andy cried. "What do you s'pose is in here?"

"I don't see anything special. It's just rock—and some dirt on the floor. But it sure is interesting."

Andy's eyes fell on something on the floor of the cave, in one corner.

"Bones!" he said. "Let's get out of here."

"They're nothing to be afraid of," Phil told him. "I'll bet they're a bear's bones. Probably been here a long time. That bear can't hurt us."

"Of course not, but couldn't there be live animals in here somewhere?"

"How could there be any, with the cave closed? Didn't we have to work hard to open it? But let's see what else is in here."

He flashed the light against the walls and up against the roof.

"There's a shelf of rock on that side," he said. "It would make a good bed if a person had to hide here."

"Maybe that is where those thieves slept, that Mr. Lane told us about."

"Maybe," Phil agreed. "Say, this cave would be a good place to hide things. See all the little nooks and crevices along the walls."

Andy wasn't much interested in them. He hadn't any idea of trying to hide anything, but Phil seemed quite excited over them.

"I wonder how far this cave goes back," said Andy.

"Not so very far," said Phil. "I think that back wall is the end of it. I guess this room is the whole cave."

It was an irregular room, with some big rocks in one corner at the back.

"We can have a lot of fun here," said Andy. "We'd better bring a lantern or two next time, so we can have more light. Let's go home now."

Phil was still flashing the beam of light up on the walls, as if he were hunting for something.

"Yes, we'd better go," he said. "But we'll come again soon."

As they were starting toward the entrance there came to their ears a familiar sound—a whining sound.

"There's Ponto," Andy exclaimed. "I didn't let him come with me, but he's followed our tracks."

He gave his usual whistle. Ponto appeared at the doorway.

"We're coming," said Andy.

Ponto didn't seem to want to come in. "I guess he isn't keen on coming into such a dark place," said Phil.

He threw the beam from the flashlight once more along the walls. Then they went out through the jagged archway and hurried down to the sugarhouse. They put the flashlight in the cupboard and the tools down in the corner.

"I'll not go back to the store," said Andy. "I'll go right down home."

"What about the groceries you were to get?" Phil reminded him.

"Jeepers! I forgot all about them. I'll have to go back with you." And they made a bee line for the village.

"What luck did you have?" asked Mr. Lane, when they dashed into the store.

"Good luck," they replied together.

"We opened up the cave," Phil told him. "But we couldn't stay long enough today to find out very much. We want to go again soon."

Mr. Lane had been opening some of the boxes and cartons with the Hallowe'en things in. "Here are enough horns and whistles to make plenty of noise," he said. "There are all sorts of sounds. One mews like a cat. One barks like a dog. One growls like a bear."

"We'll have a lot of fun that night," said Andy. "But I forgot the groceries."

"Your mother telephoned about them," said the storekeeper. "I sent them by a neighbor who was driving that way."

"Oh, dear! What is my head good for?" And Andy was off like a rocket. He burst into the living-room with, "I'm awfully sorry, Mom. I did forget the groceries."

Mother laughed. "You go to the head of the class for a champion forgetter."

Joan came in with a doll in her arms. "Just see what Rosalind and I did! Isn't she the stylish lady?"

"I s'pose so. What fun can it be to dress dolls?"

But Joan and Rosalind knew.

7.　Five Dollars

MR. LANE had spread a good supper for himself in the ice cream corner, as he often did when he had to work late, and though Phil knew his supper would be waiting for him when he got home, he accepted a sandwich gratefully. While they were eating, Mr. Lane said, "I remember some more things about that cave. Those thieves left some of the stolen things in the cave, as I told you. Some of those things were quite valuable. And we were fond of them because they had been in our families a long time."

"Were they never found?"

"Not all of them. Some of them belonged to my family, some to Andy's, some to Mrs. Woodman. There were two rings that belonged to my mother, a pearl necklace to Andy's grandmother and a diamond bracelet to Mrs. Woodman. When the thieves were caught they said those things were still in the cave, and thorough search was made but nobody really believes they were left there."

"Then there's no use looking?"

"Not much, I think. But you can climb better than some of us. And if you *should* find them, you'd certainly be doing us a great favor—a favor that we'd never forget."

"I'll look carefully when I go up there again," Phil promised. "Did you send word to my uncle that I'd stay to help you tonight?"

"Yes, by a neighbor passing there."

They went to work opening the boxes of Hallowe'en goods. Phil climbed a ladder and filled one window with bright-colored paper caps and shiny horns and whistles and other noise-makers.

"This is fun," he said, as he stood off to look at the window when he was through.

"Here's a damaged noise-maker that I'll give you," said Mr. Lane.

Phil tried it.

"Thank you. It will still make a noise. Is there anything more for me to do today?"

"No; but if you want to work on Saturday, you may come all day then. That is always a busy day."

Light-hearted and happy, Phil went home to his cousin's house. Uncle John was waiting for him, sitting by the window.

He said at once, "I heard you were wasting your time going up through the woods."

Phil stopped in amazement. "I didn't think there was any harm in having a little fun. Mr. Lane didn't need me till later. Did the man tell you that I wouldn't be home?"

"Yes; and he told me about your going up to the woods. Did Mr. Lane pay you?"

"No, but he wants me to help him all day Saturday. He'll pay me then."

"Wants you for all day Saturday, eh? That's good. What time does he want you to be there?"

"At eight o'clock."

"A good long day. He ought to pay you well."

Bright and early Saturday morning Phil was at the store. "Did you have a good breakfast?" Mr. Lane demanded.

"Y-es-s. I had oatmeal and bread and—"

"Warm oatmeal?"

"No, sir, but it will do."

"It won't do. Help yourself to some hot cocoa. Did you have any orange juice?"

"No."

"There's some in the icebox. Drink a glass of it some time today. Help yourself to some doughnuts and a glass of milk."

"Thank you, Mr. Lane."

Customers came all day. Phil waited on some of them, and Mr. Lane waited on others. A man came in who didn't seem to want to buy anything, but took a seat at one side and just watched the people coming and going.

"Who is he?" Phil asked.

"He's a stranger. Been coming in every day this week. He says his name is Joe Williams. That is all I know. He seems to mean well, so I let him sit in the store."

When time for closing came, Phil found that he had a little over a dollar that Mrs. Woodman and some others had given him when he delivered groceries to them.

Mr. Lane paid him four dollars for his work that day and another dollar for the short time after school.

"Isn't that too much?" Phil asked.

"Not too much for the good work you did. And I hope you'll come next Saturday."

Phil went along the street toward Uncle John's house whistling a popular song.

"I can soon have a new sweater," he was thinking.

Uncle John was waiting. "You've had a long day," he said, when Phil had come into the living-room.

"Yes, but I liked it."

"Did Thomas Lane work you pretty hard?"

"Not too hard. I enjoyed it."

"Did he pay you well?"

Phil didn't reply at once. He was thinking, "I don't see why I have to tell." But he said, "Yes, I'm satisfied."

"How much. Out with it."

"For all day today and the short time last Monday, five dollars."

"Five dollars! That's a lot of money. Where are you going to keep it?"

Phil hadn't thought about that. "I'll find a safe place somewhere in my room."

A pleasant expression came over Uncle John's face. "Supper is ready," he said. "Mrs. Yarby left it in the oven keeping warm. I'll put it on while you wash up."

Not since Phil had come to live there had he found Uncle John so agreeable.

Phil went up to his room and put his money in a certain small drawer in the dresser, all except the coins given to him when he delivered groceries. Those he kept in his pocket.

All through supper Uncle John was pleasant. He asked about the places Phil had gone and what people he had seen in the store.

Phil sat at the table in the living-room after supper and did his homework, for his own room was not heated and the evenings were cool.

At nine o'clock, tired from the long day, he said good night and started upstairs to his room. Uncle John followed.

"You'd better let me keep that money for you," he said. "Someone might steal it if you leave it in your room."

"Oh, Uncle John, I'm sure it will be safe there. Or, if you think it won't be, I'll find some other place for it. I'd like to keep it myself."

Seeing that a pleasant way of asking didn't get it, Uncle John became cross.

"Phil, you'll hand that money over to me, or you'll not stay here any longer."

"But Uncle John, I can take care of it. I'd like it handy where I can have it to use when I need it."

"Boys aren't judges of what they really need. You'd spend it foolishly. You might even be so foolish as to think you had to have a new sweater; and that old one has a lot of wear in it yet."

"I do want a new one."

Now Uncle John became really cross. "Hand that money over to me, Phil, without any more fuss."

Reluctantly, Phil opened the little drawer and took out the five-dollar bill and handed it to Uncle John.

Long after he had put out the light, Phil lay awake thinking over his problem.

8.　　Winter Fun

THE FIRST snow came early that year. Next Saturday
morning Joan heard Mother call, "Joan! Joan! Time
to get up! It's nearly nine o'clock."

"Nine o'clock! Late for school," thought Joan, as
she hopped out of bed and dressed quickly.

Andy was eating breakfast when she came downstairs. "Both of us late," gasped Joan.

"Don't you remember what day it is?" Andy asked.

"Why, it's Friday, isn't it? We'll be late. The bus must have gone. Why didn't you call me earlier, Mother?"

Mother only smiled. Andy said, "This isn't Friday, Goosey. Didn't the teacher say yesterday, 'Good-bye till Monday?' "

"Oh, yes. I guess I slept too hard last night. It's Saturday. What are we going to do today?"

"Look outdoors and you'll see."

Ponto followed her to the window as she looked out with astonished eyes. "Good! It's been snowing."

"Yes, and the snow is deep enough to make good sliding on the hill."

"I'll put on my snowsuit as soon as I finish breakfast."

Andy ran out to the garage, where the sleds had been stored since last spring. Then he went down cellar for shovels.

"What are the shovels for?" Joan asked.

"To pack the snow down. We have to pack it hard or our sleds won't slide very far on this first snow."

Each one carrying a shovel and pulling a sled, they started off across the hillside. Ponto trotted happily along, sometimes going off to chase a bird or a rabbit.

The hillside was a beautiful sight that morning. Snow lay deep on the ground and covered every bush and tree. The branches of the evergreens were bent down with the weight of it.

"It looks like fairyland," said Joan. "Is the snow deep enough for the sleds to go nicely?"

"Yes, after we've packed it down."

About halfway across the hillside there was a long slope, down which a wagon track had once gone.

"Here's where we'll make the slide," said Andy. "Here will be the top of it, by this big rock."

With his shovel he began to pound down hard on the soft new snow, making a track wide enough for the sleds. "Look, Joan! See how I do it. You can help too."

She took her shovel and went to work with a will. She found the work a bit hard but fun.

Soon she said, "You go ahead, Andy, and mark out the path and I'll smooth down this next part."

For the next half-hour they were busy slapping the shovels down on the feathery snow, till they had a good slide part way down the hill.

Meanwhile, Ponto ran off, came back and stood watching them, then whisked off again and scared a flock of snowbirds so they flew away.

"Gee! This is hard work," said Andy, as he looked down at the part still left to do before they would reach the bottom of the hill.

"Let's go to the sugarhouse and get a bite to eat," said Joan.

"Sure we'll go up there, but I want to take one slide first."

With that he picked up his sled, ran a few feet, plunked it down on the smooth snow and stretched out on it. Down he sped, down, down the hill, nearly to the foot of it.

"Hurrah!" he shouted to Joan. "It's a grand hill. Come on down."

Joan did as she had seen him do, plunked her sled down on the ground and was carried swiftly down the hill."

"That's a dandy hill," she said. "Only it's not long enough."

"After we've been up to the sugarhouse and got something to eat, we'll come back and finish it clear down to the fence.

Leaving their sleds at the top of the hill, they trudged through the snow to the sugarhouse. Joan went first to the cupboard and took down the package of raisins she had brought one day. She held it out to Andy, who took a handful.

"How about the cookies?" he asked. "I'm hungry enough to eat a dozen."

Joan took off the cover of the cooky jar and looked

in. "What has become of the cookies?" she exclaimed. "They're gone again!"

"Jeepers! You don't say so!"

"Someone must have been here and found our cooky jar. I wonder who," said Joan.

"Maybe that stranger," said Andy.

He went over to see if the window was still fastened. "It is just as I left it," he reported. "And the nuts seem to be all here too."

"I'm glad they were left," said Joan.

"Let's go back to the hill," said Andy.

He was fastening the door when Joan asked, "Where's Ponto?"

Andy whistled for the dog. They waited a few more moments for him to come. But no dog came happily running in answer to that call.

"Such a bothersome dog," said Andy. "Never around when we want him."

But in a moment they heard him barking somewhere back of the sugarhouse. It sounded as if he might be in the thick clump of evergreens up the hill.

Andy whistled again—over and over. By this time Ponto was growling and snarling at something.

"I wonder why he is growling so loud," said Joan.

"He is telling someone that he doesn't like him. That is Ponto's way," Andy told her.

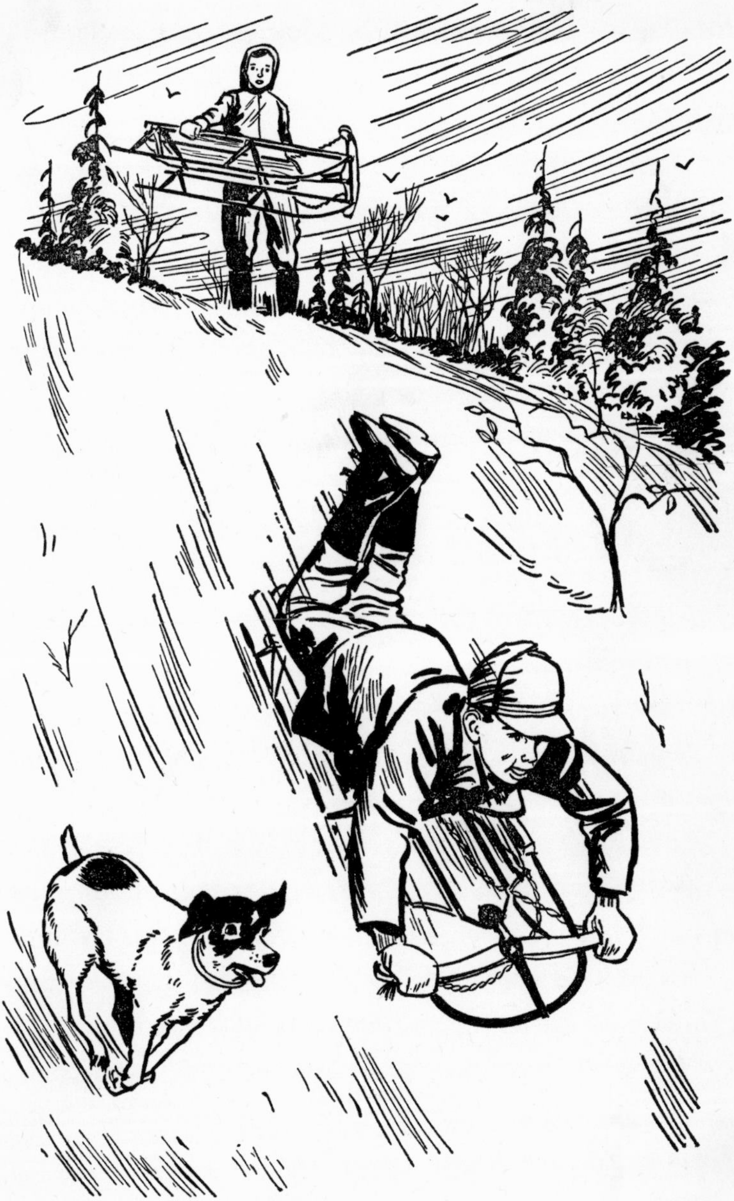

"I wonder who," Joan said.

In another moment Ponto came running around the corner of the building; and the three of them went down to the hill.

But Andy couldn't get out of his mind the question—Who was Ponto growling at? "I'll bet it is the same man that kicked him," he thought.

As they came to the edge of the woods they saw a number of boys and girls on the hill.

"Jeepers! Just see all the kids on our hill," said Andy.

Several boys and girls had brought their sleds and were shouting and having a jolly time sliding down the hill.

Joan caught sight of Rosalind and waved to her. Andy looked for Phil, but he wasn't there.

"Hello, everybody!" Andy shouted, waving his hand to them.

"We thought you wouldn't mind if we took some slides on your hill," said Tom Jackson.

"Of course not. The more the merrier," Andy assured him.

"It's a grand hill," said Mary Brenton. Her cheeks were rosy and her eyes were shining.

Andy got his sled and started down. He went faster than anyone else, for he took a long run to start with.

"You fellows have made the hill better," he said, when he reached the bottom. "So many sleds have made it smoother than we could with shovels."

Rosalind and Joan kept together, going down one after the other, laughing when they reached the foot of the long hill and tumbled off into the snow.

After a while, Phil came along, having delivered some groceries near by. He stood by the fence till Andy came down.

"What do you think that stranger is doing these days?" said Phil speaking in a low tone so no one else would hear. "He's going up toward your sugar-house almost every day."

"Why is he going there?" asked Andy.

"Maybe he isn't going into it, but he sneaks off through the woods in that direction. I see him when I'm out delivering groceries. I suspect he's up to no good," said Phil.

They talked a few minutes longer, then Andy said, "Can't you come to the hill for some fun this afternoon?"

"I'd like to, but I must keep busy on my job. So long. I'll be seeing you Monday on the bus. And let's go to the cave again if it's a good day."

"All right. So long." He went back to the store; while Andy joined the frolickers on the hill.

9. Strange Sounds

WHEN SCHOOL was out the following Monday, Phil and Andy walked along together to the school bus waiting at the curb.

"Are we going to the cave today?" Andy asked.

"If I'm not needed at the store. I'll telephone you from there."

When they reached the village, he left his books in

his room at Uncle John's and hurried on to the store.

"Do you need me this afternoon, Mr. Lane?" he asked.

"No; if you have anything else you'd like to do, I can manage alone."

"It's the cave. Andy and I'd like to go there again."

"A good idea. I hope you'll have the good luck to find some of those old things I told you about."

"I'll hunt for them. And now may I telephone to Andy?"

"Certainly."

As he came away from the phone, Phil noticed that the stranger came in at the door and stopped at the counter where the horns and whistles were kept. Phil thought he put out his hand to take one, but drew it back quickly.

Phil nodded to him, hurried out and rushed along the street. He had to go slower when he came to the fields, for there was no path in the snow.

When he came to the sugarhouse, Andy was already there. "I brought two lanterns," he said. "It's awful dark in that cave. And we'll take the flashlight too."

They lighted the lanterns before starting, although the sun was shining brightly. "It will be nice to have them already lighted when we go in," said Phil.

Walking over the snowy ground with lighted lanterns on a bright sunny day might have looked queer if there had been anyone around to see them, but they seemed to be the only persons up there.

Phil went into the cave first; and soon they were both in the dark room underground. Andy hung his lantern on a sharp corner of rock. Phil put his on the shelf.

"First, let's find out whether this is the whole cave," said Phil, after they had made sure there was no one in there but themselves.

Taking their lanterns, they walked around all sides, swinging the lights into dark corners, going around curves in the walls, for the cave was very irregular.

In one corner of the wall at the back they did discover a sort of passage that might lead to another room, but they couldn't find any opening at the end of it.

"I guess this one big room is all there is," said Phil.

"I'm glad of it," said Andy. "I wouldn't like to think that there might be some person or animal hiding in another part to pop out at us."

Phil held his lantern up high. "I believe there is a little opening up there above our heads," he said. "It's too small for us to crawl through."

"There sure is," said Andy. "I wonder what it leads to."

"Let's write our names on the wall," Phil suggested.

"And the date," said Andy. "Then folks that come here will know that we were here first."

No sooner said than done. With a stubby pencil they proudly wrote the two names in big letters.

"I guess this is just an old bear cave," said Phil. "And surely there aren't any bears here now—nothing but those bones."

Andy glanced at the pile of bones and shivered.

"I want to see what's up along the walls," said Phil, having in mind his promise to Mr. Lane to look for those old treasures.

He climbed up on the shelf of rock. "Gee! There's an old blanket here!" he exclaimed. "Someone must have slept here sometime."

"Is it very old?" Andy asked.

"Not ragged at all. And it looks quite clean. Queer, isn't it?"

"There are a lot of queer things here," said Andy, a little later. "Look at this!"

He held something he had picked up from the floor. "Look! Here's a dime!"

"I'll be jiggered," said Phil, from his perch on the

shelf of rock. "It must be very old, for this cave has been closed—lost, for so many years."

Andy held the coin close to the flashlight. "It's only 1948!" he exclaimed. "This couldn't have been left by the robbers."

"I'll be twice jiggered," said Phil. "Now who's been prowling around here?"

Andy stood open-mouthed, holding the telltale coin.

"I'll be right down," said Phil.

But he took time to poke his hands into some little nooks and crevices, partly to find out whether there was anything there, partly to find where there was a good place to hide something, if ever he wanted to.

"Listen! I hear something," Andy said, in a loud whisper.

It was a strange fluttering sound and seemed to come from the ceiling.

Phil threw the beam of the flashlight up there. "Bats! They live in caves."

Something flew past Andy's head, something black and furry. He ducked and brushed it away.

"Let's get out of here," he said. "I don't like bats in my hair."

Phil started to come down. Andy stood listening to something.

"I hear a growl, Phil. Maybe there *is* a bear in here."

It sounded as if it were in the back part of the cave, near the wall.

"Let's get out of here quick," Andy exclaimed.

Phil came down. The growl grew louder and louder. It seemed to fill the cave with that frightening noise.

"Let's beat it," said Phil. "Maybe there's one coming in through some passage that we haven't found."

He grabbed one lantern and Andy the other. In a few seconds they were out in the sunshine.

"It's surely queer," said Phil. "Could there be a live bear in that cave?"

They talked about it as they followed their footprints to the sugarhouse. There they left the flashlight and one of the lanterns.

"I'll take the other lantern down to the house," said Andy.

"Let's not tell anyone about that bear's growl—not yet," said Phil.

Two days later there came a heavy snowstorm. All one night and day the white flakes came down. Andy didn't go to school that day. Phil got off the bus at the Draper place to find out what was the matter with his chum.

He had to wade through deep snow to reach the porch.

"Where's Andy?" he asked when Mrs. Draper came to the door.

"He has a cold and so had to stay at home today. In fact, he's in bed."

"I'm awfully sorry. The teacher wanted me to find out. Tell him I hope he'll be well soon. I'll be seeing him. Good day."

Mrs. Draper called after him. "Phil, I need someone to clear the walks. With Mr. Draper in New York and Andy in bed—would you want to do it?"

"Sure. Where's a shovel?"

With a will he went to work. Throwing the masses of sparkling white snow to the sides, he worked till he had done all the walks. There was the front walk, the walk to the side door, the one to the back door and to the garage. It took him about an hour.

When he went to the door to see if there was anything more he could do to help, Mrs. Draper said, "You've done a grand job. How much do I owe you?"

"Oh, Mrs. Draper, I don't want any pay. You folks have been so good to me that I'm glad to find something I can do for you."

"But I engaged you, Phil. I meant to pay you all the time. Would two dollars be enough?"

"I wouldn't think of taking that much."

"Well, a dollar and a half. You really must take something or I won't feel like letting you do it again."

"If that is the way you feel about it, I'll take one dollar."

He went down toward the village with a happy heart. Here was some more money of his very own, some that Uncle John couldn't claim.

He put the bill into a wallet that his mother had given him and walked proudly down to the store, as happy a lad as there was in that town.

10.   Bread and Water

NOVEMBER days passed happily for the next two weeks. Andy was soon able to go to school. Joan and Rosalind were busy after school, sliding on the hill or dressing dolls or making things for Christmas.

Phil shoveled many a walk and tucked dollar bills into his wallet and coins into a little bag, then took them to a certain place on the hill and hid them, all except a few that he kept for ice cream.

The stranger still sat around the store a few hours every day. "It's queer that he doesn't tell what he does or where he lives," Mr. Lane said one day to Phil. "But as long as he seems to be harmless and doesn't do any damage, I let him sit here."

"I suspect he's up to no good," said a customer. "I wouldn't trust him far."

When Mr. Draper came home one Saturday afternoon, he asked, "What are you doing these days, Andy?"

"School."

"Oh, yes, of course. But after school?"

"We have fun on the hill. The boys and girls come there after school and we slide till dark. But some days Phil and I go off by ourselves. We've found an old cave."

Mr. Draper was at once interested. "That cave up in the cliff?"

"Yes. We had to dig away dirt and stones and bushes and vines."

"Good. What is it like?"

"Just one big room underground—all dark inside —with a bear's bones in one corner."

"How do you know they are a bear's bones?"

"Phil said they were. That's all I know."

"I'd like to see that cave. Some day when I'm home

I'll go up there with you. It's been closed up ever since I have been coming here."

But that week-end was rainy and they put it off till another time.

The Tuesday before Thanksgiving came. When Phil went home that afternoon, after helping the grocer for an hour, Uncle John said at once, "So you've been earning extra money and keeping it yourself. I've heard about your shoveling walks and doing errands. Hand that money over to me."

"Oh, Uncle John, please! I earned it myself by working extra. I want to keep that. You have all the rest."

"You'll hand it to me, I say. I'll give back enough for the things you really need; but you must let me handle it."

Phil thought of the new sweater he wanted. He thought of the extra pair of shoes he needed.

"Get it right now, before supper," said Uncle John.

"It isn't here. I can't get it tonight."

"Isn't here? Have you been hiding it somewhere?"

Phil nodded.

How hungry he was that night! It seemed as if he couldn't wait till they would sit down to the table. The good smell of roast beef and pumpkin pie that

Mrs. Yarby had left in the kitchen for them came drifting into the room.

"Very well," said Uncle John. "If you can't get the money, it's bread and water till you do."

Phil lay awake a long time that night, thinking and planning. His heart was bitter.

The next morning he got up early and packed a small satchel with a few things—socks, underwear, handkerchiefs, two books and a few little keepsakes he had brought from home.

Early, before Uncle John was up, he took it to the front porch and hid it under an old couch.

Mr. Lane had said the day before, "I wish you would help me all day tomorrow. The day before Thanksgiving is the busiest day of the year for me."

So Uncle John knew that he was going to the store that morning and would ask no questions when he saw Phil turn toward the village. But what if he saw the satchel?

His breakfast of bread and water over, he went the same as usual along the walk at the side of the house, but this time he went up on the front porch.

Taking the satchel from under the couch, he walked to the street between high banks of snow, which he had tossed up when he cleared the walks.

When he reached the sidewalk, fortunately the high snowbanks by the fence would prevent anyone in the house from seeing what he was carrying. Only his head and shoulders showed above the snow.

Uncle John was watching at the dining-room window. "I wonder if I've been too hard on him," he was thinking.

Phil didn't feel too happy about it. He had always tried to do things openly. He gave one last look at the fine old house before he came to the bend in the road that shut it from view. As he walked along he remembered the money he had hidden.

"I must be sure to go for it before I start away," he said to himself over and over. "That's all I'll have for food on the trip."

On coming into the store, he slipped the satchel into a corner of the back room before Mr. Lane could see it.

"Good morning," said the storekeeper, when Phil came back into the front part. "Are you ready for a big day's work today?"

"Sure."

Mr. Lane noticed that he looked white. "How about breakfast?" he asked.

"I had some."

"You don't have to tell me you didn't have much.

Go to the icebox and get some milk. Make yourself a cup of hot chocolate and eat some bread and butter. Take a doughnut from that box that is open."

As Phil went to do it, the storekeeper looked after him. "I wonder what John Davison has been up to now," he thought. "The old curmudgeon! But I didn't think even he would skimp a boy on food."

It was a busy day. Customers came in and bought twice as much as usual, for they were going to have lots of company on Thanksgiving Day. But once Phil had some good food, he didn't care how much he had to do.

"Help yourself to a banana and another glass of milk," said Mr. Lane in the middle of the morning.

"Thank you, Mr. Lane."

Soon after lunch the stranger, Joe Williams, came in. He took his usual seat by the stove. "It's cold up on the hillside today," he said.

That was the first time he had ever mentioned where he spent his time when he was not in the store. Mr. Lane looked over in surprise. "What were you doing up on the hill?"

"Well—I was just looking for something. Fact is, I heard there was some treasure left in that cave a long time ago. I thought I might as well have it as anyone else—if I could find it."

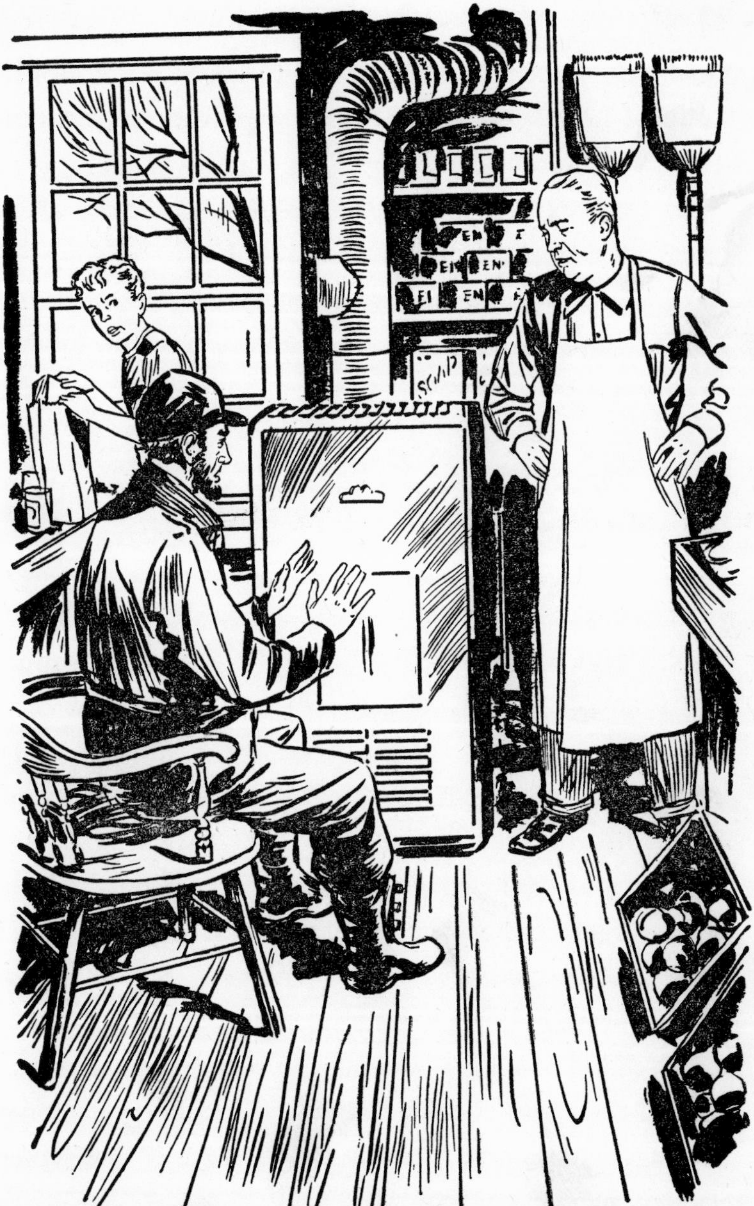

He looked over at Phil, who was busy putting a large order of groceries into a bag.

"So that is what made him hang around here all these weeks," thought Mr. Lane. Aloud he said, "Have you found the cave? The entrance of that old cave has been lost for many years."

"Sure I've found it. I've found two entrances—one over beyond the ridge."

"You don't say. I didn't know there were two."

"A long passage leads from one to the other," said the stranger. "But never a bit of treasure can I find at either end."

Mr. Lane came over to the stove. "You're wasting your time trying to find any treasure in that cave. Every crevice was searched long ago. There can't be anything left there."

A few minutes later, when Phil was going past, he saw the man reach over and take a pair of mittens from a shelf.

"You'd better put those back," he said. "If you don't, I'll have to report you to Mr. Lane."

"I was just looking at them," he explained. Then he put them back and left the store.

By the middle of the afternoon they were not so busy. Most of the customers had been there in the forenoon. Phil was hoping for a chance to tell Mr.

Lane something; and this seemed a good time.

"Mr. Lane, may I buy a sweater? And will you take it out of my pay tonight?"

"Sure. But maybe you can find a good sweater in the back room. That wouldn't cost you anything. Sometimes folks get a new one and leave their old one. And I put them back there. Some of them are pretty good. Help yourself."

"Thank you, but I want a new sweater—one that looks good and is warm. I'd rather buy one."

"All right. Go ahead and pick one out."

He found one that just suited him and put it on.

"If I could find a pair of shoes in the back room, I'd like to," he said.

"Help yourself," said Mr. Lane.

He found a pair that seemed about right. "I don't know why anyone threw those away," he said. They were a bit too long, but otherwise they fitted.

He tucked the shoes and the old sweater into the satchel, then surprised Mr. Lane by saying, "I'm going away from here. I won't be coming after today."

"Why, Phil, what's the trouble?"

"I can't stand it at Uncle John's any longer. And I won't."

"Oh, but to run away—Tell me all about it, lad."

"All right; but I've made up my mind."

11.   Running Away

PHIL stood there a few moments, not wanting to begin.

"Tell me all about it, Phil," again said Mr. Lane kindly.

"Uncle John has taken all the money you have paid me; and now he wants what I've earned shoveling walks and doing errands. And I've had nothing to eat there but bread and water since yesterday morning."

The words came out fast, now that the lad was started.

"Why didn't you tell me, Phil? I'd have given you all you wanted to eat."

"I didn't want to tattle. And you did give me plenty."

"But you mustn't run away, Phil," said Mr. Lane in a kind voice. "You have many friends here. My wife and I would like you to come and live with us."

"I can't do that. Uncle John would make trouble for anyone who helped me. I'm sure he would make me go back to his house. I can't stay in the village."

"But where will you go? You haven't any other relatives who would take you into their home, have you?"

"Maybe I'll go down to New York, maybe Boston. I'll hitchhike."

"But you mustn't do this, Phil. You don't know anyone in New York. You couldn't get a job there, young as you are. You'd starve."

"I'll manage some way, Mr. Lane. I just won't ever go back to Uncle John's. I brought my things away this morning."

"Oh, dear!" said Mr. Lane.

"I don't like to go away from you," Phil declared. "And I hate to leave Andy and Joan and that fine school."

"Listen to me, Phil. Change your mind. Stay with us and I'll manage your uncle. I'll tell John Davison what I think of him."

Phil stood there with a troubled look on his face. Then he spoke slowly and firmly, "Thank you very much, Mr. Lane. But I'm going soon, so as to get far on my way before dark."

Mr. Lane had to go to wait on a customer, who took a long time. Before that one went, others came in. When they were gone he looked around for Phil.

But the lad had left the store and started south along Main Street, out of the village and along the country road.

When he was quite sure that no one was following him, he stopped by the roadside and held up his thumb for a ride. That car went speeding by.

The next car went speeding past, paying no attention to him. A dozen cars went past without slowing up.

"Why doesn't one of them let me have a ride," he wondered.

He saw another one coming and made up his mind

to wave his hand and shout at the top of his voice.

But before it reached him, he remembered something. He put his hand in his pocket.

"Jeepers! I forgot to go up on the hill and get that money I hid there. How could I forget? I just can't go without it."

He picked up his satchel and went back part way to the village, then walked through the fields up toward the cliff. It was hard walking in the deep snow, but he kept on till he nearly reached the cliff.

"I'll get the money out of its hiding place, then I'll hurry back," he was thinking.

But the sun was nearly down and dusk was coming in the woods.

"I'd better wait till morning," he decided. "But where shall I sleep tonight?"

Then a bright idea came to him. "Just the place," he decided. "I'm sure Mr. Draper wouldn't mind."

Coming to the sugarhouse, he remembered that Andy had put a padlock on the door. He went to the window at the back.

"If I can only turn that catch, I can open the window," he said to himself.

It didn't take long to thrust the blade of his knife between the window and the frame. He was soon able to push the catch up and open the window.

Putting his satchel through first, he climbed over the sill and locked the window.

"Jeepers! This is good luck!" he exclaimed aloud. "The hayloft will be a grand place to sleep for one night."

Rays of light were still coming through the cracks, but the first thing he did was to go to the cupboard and get the flashlight.

"I'll need it later," he thought.

Turning around, he noticed the hickory nuts on the floor.

"What good luck!" he exclaimed. "I know Andy and Joan won't care if I eat a few for my supper."

He found a hammer and had cracked and eaten a few of them when he heard voices. "The boys and girls must be over on the hill. Wish I was there," he said to himself.

He had eaten a few more when he realized that the voices sounded nearer.

"Jeepers! Double jeepers! Are they coming here?" he exclaimed.

He did some quick thinking. Grabbing the satchel and the flashlight, he climbed the ladder to the loft. "They mustn't find me," was his thought. "They would never let me go away."

At the far side of the loft he discovered a hollow in the hay. Working fast, he made it deeper and lay down in it, then pulled more hay over him and covered up the satchel.

"What could be nicer?" he thought. "I'm as snug as a bug in a rug."

When they came in, he heard three voices. "Rosalind must have come with them," he decided. "It's a good thing it's getting darker all the time."

He heard Joan exclaim, "Someone has eaten some of the hickory nuts!"

"No one could get in here," Andy told her. "The door was locked when we came and the window is locked."

"What became of those nuts then?" asked Joan. "I guess I know when some have been cracked. Here are the shells on the hearth."

She took up the hammer and asked Rosalind if she liked hickory nuts.

"Indeed I do."

"I'll crack you some." With that Joan cracked a few nuts for herself and Rosalind.

Andy was thinking. "How could anyone have come in here, eaten some of the hickory nuts and got out again? The door is locked and the window catch is turned crosswise. It surely is a mystery."

The light was fading fast. "I'm going up on the loft to see if everything is all right there, then we'll go home," he said.

Joan had just reached into the cupboard for the flashlight and Andy was about to step on the first rung of the ladder when there burst forth a terrible sound—a sound so weird and loud and altogether dreadful that the girls ran to the door in terror.

"What could it be?" Rosalind asked, when they were outside.

"How do I know?" said Joan. "If I believed in giants I would think a giant was in the sugarhouse and was yelling at the top of his voice."

One couldn't tell from what direction the sound came, for it seemed to fill the old building and even to come from the sky above it.

Andy went no further up the ladder. He followed the girls, quickly closed the door and locked it. "We'd better beat it," he said.

All three scooted away from the building and across the hillside. "What could that horrible sound have been? Who could have made it?" Joan asked when, half-way home, they stopped for breath.

"I'll be jiggered," said Andy. "It sounded like the horns we heard at Hallowe'en, only louder. That stranger must have been somewhere around. He couldn't have been inside the sugarhouse, for no one could have got in there, with the door locked and the window fastened from the inside."

Rosalind said good-bye and went home without going in. They found Father at home.

"Home for Thanksgiving," he said. "I wouldn't want to miss the fine dinner Mother is preparing for tomorrow. And what would Thanksgiving be if we couldn't all be together?"

"Oh, Father, we've had a scare—a great scare," said Joan. "Up in the sugarhouse. There's something awful there."

"What's that? Something in our old sugarhouse—scaring folks away?"

They both tried to tell him at once. "I'll bet it's that stranger who's been hanging around the store," said Andy.

"Maybe he's been sleeping in our sugarhouse," said Joan.

"I'll go up there with you in the morning, Andy," Father promised.

"That's grand. You'll find out if anyone can."

"I wouldn't mind someone using our sugarhouse

for shelter, but I want to know who it is. We'll find out, Andy."

The telephone rang. Andy ran to answer it. Mr. Lane was on the phone.

"Have you heard the news?" he asked.

"No, we haven't heard any special news," said Andy. "What is it?"

"Phil has run away. He has left the village."

"Phil run away? But why? Where has he gone?"

"That I don't know. I only know that he said he was going. And he was seen in the road trying to catch a ride."

Andy called Father to the phone. "Mr. Lane wants to speak to you. Phil has run away."

They heard Father saying, "If only we had known that he was so unhappy there, we'd have given him a home with us."

"Of course," said Mother, overhearing what was said. "He could have had the west bedroom."

Father talked a little longer, then came back to his favorite chair under the lamp.

"It is too bad," he said. "I sometimes wondered how long he could stand it with John Davison. If only we had known! But it is too late now."

"Why didn't Phil tell me?" asked Andy. "Joan and I would have been glad to give up that big room in the old wing so he could have a nice home."

"Of course," said Joan.

When Andy said goodnight and started upstairs, Father said, "Be ready to go with me in the morning by eight o'clock at the latest, Andy."

"All right. Call me in time and I'll be ready."

12.   A Surprise

PHIL was so tired and the soft hay made such a comfortable bed, that when he wakened the next morning the sun was shining brightly through the cracks of the old sugarhouse.

"Jeepers! I've overslept," he said to himself.

He looked at his watch. "Double jeepers! It's nearly nine o'clock."

He threw off the hay, brushed it from his clothes and dug out the satchel. Then he spied the horn with which he had scared the children the night before.

"I might need it again," he chuckled. And he put it in the satchel.

"I'd better eat a little breakfast," he decided.

He cracked some nuts and ate them.

All this hadn't taken much time, but he hurried out through the window, knowing the door was padlocked on the outside.

He had put the long shoes on, the pair he had picked up at the grocer's. "If anyone follows my footprints, he'll never mistrust whose they are in these long shoes," he said to himself.

Once more he was starting off, just as soon as he could get his money from its hiding place in the cave; and this time he wouldn't have to come back for anything. These were his thoughts as he walked up toward the cave through the sparkling snow.

Never looking back, he was almost at the cave when he heard a twig snap behind him. He looked quickly around.

There stood the stranger, Joe Williams.

"Why are you following me?" Phil demanded.

"I—I wasn't following you, not on purpose. I

was just going to the cave to hunt once more for that treasure that was hid here years and years ago. I've heard that it's never been found."

"Yes, I guess you are right. But I'd like to know how you knew about that old treasure."

"I might as well tell you, for I'm going away from this place and never come back. I know about it because a feller told me. And he was a cousin of one of the thieves."

"Oh!" said Phil.

"I came up here this morning for the last time. I thought this was a fine big cave, but I see it is only an old bear's cave. I did find another entrance though, around the curve. There's a long passage which connects with this one, but the opening between them isn't large enough for a man to crawl through."

"Is that where you stood when you made that growling sound that scared us?" Phil asked.

The stranger nodded. "And now good-bye. I'm off."

Phil watched the man start down the hill; then he went into the cave to get the few dollars he had hidden there.

"After I get that, I'll start right away," he said to himself.

Leaving the satchel on the floor of the cave, he took the flashlight and climbed up onto the wide ledge. He took the wallet out of its niche and slipped it into his pocket.

Instead of getting down at once, he put his hand here and there into crevices, farther than he had ever tried to reach before.

He was holding to a projection of rock when it broke off. Down he tumbled to the floor.

"Jeepers! I'm glad I didn't break a leg or my head," he thought, as he slowly picked himself up.

He looked up to see what had happened and discovered an old piece of cloth that had been brought to sight when the piece of rock broke off.

He climbed up on the shelf and pulled it out of the crevice. "An old bandanna handkerchief," he said to himself. "But what's wrapped up inside of it?"

The handkerchief was old and faded and dusty. Phil was about to untie it when he heard voices outside the cave.

"Jeepers! Double jeepers!" he thought. "Andy and his father. I must hide."

Grabbing the satchel he hurried toward the back of the cave and hid behind one of the big rocks in one corner.

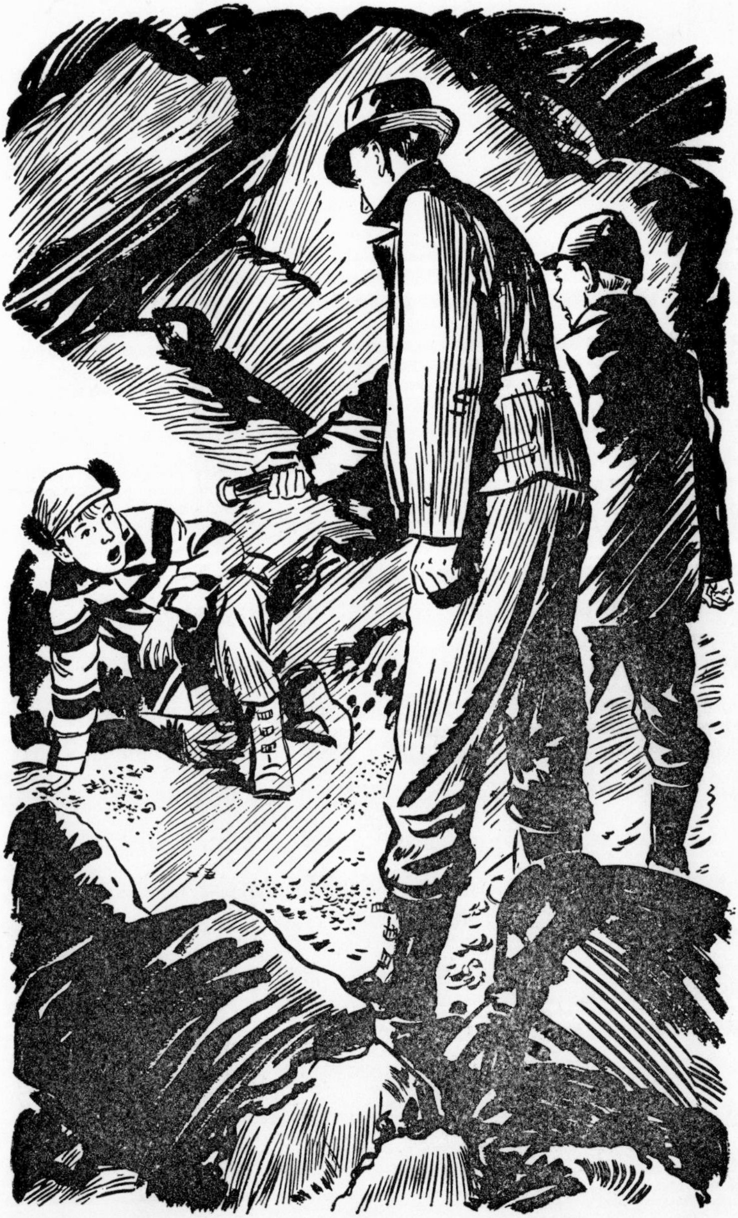

When they came into the cave, he heard Mr. Draper say, "If those footprints were made this morning, I should think we'd have found someone here."

"But there's no one here now," said Andy.

Mr. Draper stood looking around. "An interesting thing, a cave," he said. "But let's see what is in here."

He had brought a flashlight and he kept throwing the beam up on the sides of the cave.

"There are lots of nooks and crevices where small things could be hidden," he said. "Let's go toward the back and find out what's there."

He stepped toward the big rock and turned the flashlight on it. Nothing to be seen there. Then he walked around behind it. There was someone crouching behind the rock.

"Why, Phil! Hello!" Andy greeted him. "What are you doing here? We thought you had gone away."

"I was just going. I'm glad to see you, Andy, and you, Mr. Draper; but I must be going and I'm sorry you found me."

Mr. Draper spoke to him kindly. "You are surely not intending to go off and leave us, Phil. Tell us all about it. But first let's go out to the mouth of the cave."

The three of them went to the entrance and stood

there where they could look out into the bright sunlight.

"I'm going away, Mr. Draper. I just can't stand it any longer with Uncle John. So I've made up my mind to leave here and never come back."

"Oh, Phil, don't!" Andy pleaded.

Mr. Draper looked thoughtful for a moment. Then he said, "How about coming to live with us, Phil?"

"That would be grand, but my uncle wouldn't let me. And I won't go back to him."

"Perhaps you needn't. Andy and I would like you to come and live with us. And I'm sure Mother and Joan would like it too."

"Do you really mean it?" Phil asked, his face lighting up at the thought.

"Sure," Andy declared. "Of course we mean it."

"Yes, indeed," said Mr. Draper. "And now let's go down to the house and talk things over."

When they came to the sugarhouse, Andy asked, "Were you the one that blew the horn last night when the girls and I were here?"

"Yes, I was up in the hay and I was afraid you'd find me and spoil my plan for running away."

"It surely did scare us," said Andy.

When they were walking down the hillside, Phil

recalled what he had found. He pulled the bandanna out of his pocket.

"Here's something I found away up in a niche on the wall of the cave," he said. "There's something hard in it. I don't know what."

He handed Mr. Draper the old handkerchief. "We'll untie it when we get to the house," said Father.

Joan was looking out of the window. "Just see who's coming back with Dad and Andy!" she called.

Mother came over to the window. "Phil! But I thought he had run away."

Joan ran to the door and opened it when the three came up on the porch.

"Here's Phil," said Andy happily. "We got there just in time."

"In time for what?" Joan asked.

"To keep him from running away. He's going to live with us."

"Good morning, Mrs. Draper," said Phil. "Hello, Joan!"

"Phil has changed his mind," said Mr. Draper. "What would you think, Mother, of asking him to live with us?"

"Surely," Mother replied heartily. "He can share

the old wing with Andy and Joan for playing and doing his homework; and he can have the west bedroom for his own."

Phil's face lighted up with a smile, and he said gratefully, "I'll shovel walks and do errands and help whenever I'm needed."

"What have you in that old rag?" Joan asked.

"Oh, I forgot that in the excitement of welcoming Phil," said Father. "This is something he found this morning high up on one of the walls of the cave. Let's see what's in it."

He found it hard to untie the knots of such an old piece of cloth, so Mother suggested that they cut it. "It's so old and soiled that it isn't good for anything," she said.

Taking the scissors, she cut the handkerchief; and there came to view the most astonishing things.

"Jewels!" exclaimed Joan. "Beautiful jewels!"

"There's the pearl necklace that was my mother's," exclaimed Mrs. Draper. "It was stolen by those thieves twenty years ago."

She handled it lovingly. The pearls were dull after all those years. "I'll take it to the jeweler to be cleaned," she said.

Mr. Draper telephoned to Mr. Lane. "I have good

news," he said. "Phil is back and is going to live with us."

"That surely is good news," said the storekeeper. "He's as promising a boy as ever lived in this village. Tell him to come to see me soon."

"I have more news," said Mr. Draper. "I've been told that those thieves took some rings that belonged in your family."

"Yes, two rings that belonged to my mother. One was set with a ruby, one with a diamond."

"Those are like the ones Phil found in the cave."

"You don't say!" exclaimed Mr. Lane. "I'll surely be glad to have them again. They are not only valuable, but she cares for them because they were heirlooms—were handed down to her from her grandmother."

Then Mrs. Draper telephoned to Mrs. Woodman that a bracelet had been found in the cave. "It is a very handsome one—a gold one set with diamonds. Could it be yours?"

"That is just like the one those thieves stole," she said. "I'll be so happy to have it again."

Later in the day, Mr. Draper went to see Phil's uncle. "I have good news. Phil's back."

"So he's back, is he? I guess he found out that this place is not so bad. When will he be coming back here?"

"He doesn't want to come back."

"Oh, now, I guess he found that this place looked good to him when he didn't have any place to sleep."

"That wasn't it. He had to come back to get something, and I'm glad to say we found him before he got away again. I've come to ask you if you'll be willing for him to live and play and go to school with our young folks."

"He was left in my care. I s'pose I've got to keep him till he's through school."

"No, you don't have to keep him. We'd really like to have him. I'll look after him as if he were my own son."

"Eh! What's that?"

"You don't really want him, so why not let him live with us?"

Mr. Davison seemed to be thinking it over. "Well, I'm willing. In fact, I'm glad to wash my hands of him. Boys are a nuisance."

"There's a difference of opinion about that. We don't think so. And we'd enjoy having Phil as part of our family."

"All right, all right. But I'll not give up that money his mother gave me for looking after him, nor what the grocer paid him."

Mr. Draper looked him in the eye. "All right. Keep the money, but you must sign a paper releasing Phil to us. Will you do that?"

"Yes."

"And if I know Phil," said Mr. Draper, "he'll be coming to see you often and will be willing to help you any way he can."

Father went back with the good news. He found the two boys shoveling snow from the driveway. "It wasn't wide enough," Phil said.

When that was done they went into the old wing to play ping-pong, while Joan sat at the table and drew a picture of their hillside in Winter.

And when they sat down to the Thanksgiving dinner of turkey with all the fixings, there was no happier boy in all Vermont than Phil Ramsay.

"It's a great Thanksgiving Day for us all," said Mother.

THE END

BOOKS BY HELEN FULLER ORTON

Hoof-Beats of Freedom
The Gold-Laced Coat
The Treasure in the Little Trunk
Mystery in the Apple Orchard
Mystery of the Hidden Book
Mystery in the Old Red Barn
Mystery Over the Brick Wall
Mystery in the Old Cave
Mystery in the Pirate Oak
Mystery Up the Winding Stair
Mystery Up the Chimney
Mystery of the Lost Letter
Mystery at the Old Place
Mystery of the Secret Drawer
Mystery at the Little Red Schoolhouse
The Secret of the Rosewood Box